For SSM

www.hmhco.com

The illustrations in this book were done digitally.
The text type was set in Chaloops and Eatwell Chubby.
The display type was set in Eatwell Chubby.

ISBN 978-0-544-94165-6

Manufactured in China
SCP 10 9 8 7 6 5 4 3 2 1
4500646971

There's a PEST in the garden!

JAN THOMAS

Houghton Mifflin Harcourt

Boston   New York

MUNCH
MUNCH

There's a **PEST**
in the garden!

He's eaten **ALL** the beans!

That **PEST** is
still in
the garden
and he's eaten
ALL the **corn!**

GULP

What's that **PEST**
going to eat **next?**

That **PEST** is still in the garden and he's eaten **ALL** the **peas!**

GULP

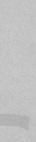

Looking for more laughs?

Get your child ready to read in three simple steps!

1 I READ	Read the book to your child.
2 WE READ	Read the book together.
3 YOU READ	Encourage your child to read the book over and over again.

CONTRA COSTA COUNTY LIBRARY